HOBO

Brian Douglas Beverly

Order this book online at www.trafford.com/05-1078
or email orders@trafford.com

Most Trafford titles are also available at major online book retailers.

Note for Librarians: A cataloguing record for this book is available from Library and Archives Canada at www.collectionscanada.ca/amicus/index-e.html

ISBN: 978-1-4120-6177-3

We at Trafford believe that it is the responsibility of us all, as both individuals and corporations, to make choices that are environmentally and socially sound. You, in turn, are supporting this responsible conduct each time you purchase a Trafford book, or make use of our publishing services. To find out how you are helping, please visit www.trafford.com/responsiblepublishing.html

Our mission is to efficiently provide the world's finest, most comprehensive book publishing service, enabling every author to experience success. To find out how to publish your book, your way, and have it available worldwide, visit us online at www.trafford.com/10510

www.trafford.com

North America & international
toll-free: 1 888 232 4444 (USA & Canada)
phone: 250 383 6864 • fax: 250 383 6804 • email: info@trafford.com

The United Kingdom & Europe
phone: +44 (0)1865 722 113 • local rate: 0845 230 9601
facsimile: +44 (0)1865 722 868 • email: info.uk@trafford.com

20 19 18 17 16 15 14 13 12 11

ACKNOWLEDGMENTS

I have been an extra in a lot of movies, I'm SAG eligible. And I've gone to Hollywood, from Tidewater, Va., in 1996. After I started with an agent in Norfolk, Va. in 1990, I came back home to Ohio, in year 2000. It once was put to me in acting workshop "How do I intend to use it in my life?" Well I thought about it, and I want to write. I believe I have the talent to write short Novels.

AUTHOR'S NOTE

The purpose of this book is to entertain you.
With adventure and drama, coming from a fiction book.

HOBO

This is a story about a man born in the late 1800's. And the 1929 Great Stock Market crash (Years of the Depression)happen for him in his small Virginian town. He is optimistic and takes to the railroad to go north, and work in a factory. "Things will be better in another town." Optimism was big in those days. It's believed that Ford Motor Company is still doing it up—to the up most. So Clarence Taylor will hop a train as hoboes do, for Toledo, Ohio.

Prologue

Horses racing up a dirt road, carrying midwives in the buggy, are on their way to Sally Taylor's house. They have just come from a farmer's town that is not too heavily populated and managed by farmers, cattlemen, and fur-traders. Sally Taylor, tossing side to side in her bed, is enduring labor pains. The fetus is out of its embryonic stage and making way for the world that will welcome a new beginner. Sally's two-room house escapes the dirt road and has its own approach, which is nothing more than a path from horses and buggy wheels coming and going. And now from off the dirt road and up the path come the three midwives.

Haddy, Jane, and Mary enter into the small, two-room house to find Sally about to have her baby. Jane goes quickly to Sally's head to soothe her. Haddy is getting at her feet so she can deliver the baby. And Mary comes from behind Haddy to get to the other side of the room. Mary, at the window, can't help but notice there hasn't been any rain for a while. It's as though they're having a drought. Crisp and dry the outdoors plant life is, because of being in the heat of the sun. Loud groans from Sally, as well as the situation, get the attention of the women. Drawing more near now, Haddy assesses Sallys condition and tries to communicate with her so that she can calm down enough to make the matter easier to deal with.

Just then, the front door bursts open, and tall in the doorway stands Barbo Brown, who had gone for the midwives. Barbo is a bald man who stands over six feet tall, heavy built, and he is in his early thirties. There in his overalls, flannel shirt, and boondocker boot shoes, he is excited to see what's going on. "Get back outside!" commands Haddy with big seriousness after she hears, looks, and sees Barbo standing there. His head touching the sky, Barbo quickly closes the door as he gets back outside.

"Hold it, Sally. Don't push anymore," says Haddy.

"I can see the head getting out," Mary, speaks up overwhelmed.

After a moment's rest, the girls get back to it, and the rest of the baby emerges, and Mary helps Haddy complete all of the tasks concerning birth from this moment forward.

Jane, trying to see, finally has to ask,

Prologue

"Is it a boy or a girl?"

"It's a boy," answers Mary.

"And listen to him crying," replies Jane.

"And he's got some lungs hasn't he?" She continues.

"Are you going to name the baby 'Clarence' after his father?" asks Mary, as she puts the newborn babe on his exhausted mother's chest.

"Don't fight to do any talking now," says Haddy.

"That's right, she needs to recover," says Jane as she gets the baby from Sally. Whispering words from Sally are saying "Yes, Clarence, It's Clarence." And all of a sudden rain is falling from the sky, without the crackling of lightning or sounds of thunder. Mary instinctively turns to the window once more and sees what she didn't hear—the light Rain Fall.

"Oh my goodness, it's raining!" bellows Mary.

"Sssh.... Hold your voice down, don't cry out so," says Jane.

Mary is excited because of seeing the near drought before, and now it's raining. Hearkened, Sally lifts her head just enough to see out of the window, whispering a word: "Rainbow." Then she falls to sleep.

Part One

Clarence Works At The Depot

1

Ten years had gone by very quickly. And Clarence Taylor had got his fathers looks. He was a tall slender build, brown-skinned man, who also was very handsome and most distinguished.

There is Sally filling the kitchen sink with dishes after she and her son Clarence both have finished eating. Sally is thinking of her late husband and how he was killed months before the baby was born. While she is lost in thought, little Clarence has to ask, "What happened to daddy again mommy?" Looking down at him with her hands in a sink full of soapy water and dirty dishes, Sally tells the story once more: "It was wild dogs. They attacked your father when he was fishing. And the bites from the dogs caused him to bleed to death. And Barbo went to meet up with your father, it was their favorite fishing spot. Barbo always takes his shotgun that has two barrels in case he sees a rabbit. When he got there the dogs were already attacking your father. So, then, he shot and killed one of the dogs. But missed with the next shot. The shotgun going off made the rest of them run away. But it was too late for your father. He bled to death before Barbo could get him out of the woods."

Teary-eyed and whimpering, Clarence has his arms and hands reaching out to his mother. Sally gives him a hug and talks him down out of his tears. Sally is five feet four inches tall-a full figured woman, who has bronzy brown skin. And she gets compliments about her good proportions. She is also very kind.

2

The hunters and trappers are going strong because it is winter. And pelts are thick with fur, which then are very well marketable. A locomotive is blowing its whistle to warn the incoming of it all, than a loud screeching is heard as the train comes to a halt. Most excitedly the townspeople gather near to see the passengers get off the train. After it has stopped, the doors to the passenger cars are opened and people spill out onto the boardwalk that leads to the depot.

It's Eighteen Ninety Eight, a time when trains are a very big mode of travel. A beautiful and stylish lady has just stepped down into the crowd of people. "Hay you there! Come for to carry me off, will you?" she shouts at a man who is middle aged with a gray beard and mustache. And within an instant, he is at her side.

"Yes um, ma'am."

"I would like you to carry my bags for me, and I'll be headed for that carriage over there, that's bound for the hotel."

"Yes um."

"Oh, and what is your name?"

"It's George, call me George, ma'am."

The stylish lady also talks with an accent that is pleasant to hear and gives George a good feeling to know that he is dealing with a foreigner rather than the attitude from a lot of the locals. By the time they get to the carriage it has filled up with passengers and their baggage. There is no room for the lady.

"Bring yourselves together, then there'll be more room," she argues.

"No we can't!" the passengers complain, "We're already crowded!"

"It looks to me that you can," she shouts back at the passengers.

"You'll have to wait until I get back," says the driver of the horses' carriage.

Sighing, and sighing again, "Ok, I'll wait," she says. Impatiently she moves backwards, to stand off from the carriage. And then it goes on its way, leaving her behind. She turns to George who has her bags, and tells him to set them down over by the depot. "I'll wait there and here is something for your effort, so you can continue on your way." After words she becomes more impatient. And she is

-watching the crowd move about and has spotted a boy standing against the building. Calling for him is too difficult. So she hurries over to where he is and tugs at his coat to get his attention. “Hay there! Hay you there!” The disruption to the ten-year-old Clarence Taylor makes him jump, because he is taken by surprise. The startled Clarence with eyes wide open turns to her nodding his head up and down, as if to be saying yes before she can ask him what she is about to. “Oh my goodness, I didn’t mean to scare you so badly. I only wish to show you my bags over there. I’ll give you a nickel to help me carry them to the hotel. I can see it's over there, two streets away,” she finishes, with two fingers pinched together-the nickel just above Clarence's head. “Yes, I’ll carry them.” The enticed young boy heaves the luggage up into his fold, and is being led to the hotel by the very beautiful and stylish woman who speaks with an accent.

The streets are full of people moving about, and lively is the business thereof, and laughter fills the air with good cheer. After entering the hotel, the duo make their way to the front desk:

"You there, I would like to get a room," she beckons the desk clerk.

And behind the front desk a not so very tall, half bald man with specs down on his nose is quick to respond:

"Will you listen at that, you're French," he answers back to her, looking over the top of his spectacles.

"Yes, Oh yes, that I am. And I'm here from Paris, by

way of the New York's." Answering up to that is just what she had wanted, so her presents could be of some importance.

"Here on business I presume?" a woman asks who's checking into the hotel along with her husband.

"Well… here is the roster for checking in, we'll have to get your name," the desk clerk buts in.

"Ok! And my name is Jacqueline Vadim. And that's right to you ma'am, I'm here on business. And it is hats to sell locally here in your town," she continued talking aloud, and could be heard throughout the hotel lobby.

"You'11 be looking up Miss Jane Somers, who has the hat shop," says the desk clerk.

"Yes, that's her name," answers Jacqueline Vadim.

"By the way, do you know where it is? Because I understand that it is near here," she continues.

"Yes, the hat shop is just down the street from here," answers the desk clerk. "And for you there's a room just above us. It has a front window, so you can view the main street," he continues. "And just how long will you be staying?" finishes the desk clerk.

"For the week. Then I must be getting back to New York for Paris," answers Jacqueline Vadim.

"Here is the key to the door and that'll be two Dollars."

Jacqueline Vadim in the lead again hurries Clarence up the stairs. And she struggles with the key for a moment before she can get the door open. And Clarence trailing in from behind her can't help but dump the luggage down onto the floor.

"Oh please do be careful with my things!" cries Jacqueline Vadim.

"I'm sorry," says Clarence.

"Never mind, it was a long carry. So here is a penny as well as your nickel."

Clarence with eyes bulging out of his head, grabs the money and without saying thanks runs out of the room, down the stairs and through the lobby.

"You better slow down young man!"

Clarence is out the door, and running down the street before the desk clerk with the spectacles can be heard. Racing down the street, Clarence Taylor is on his way to the hat shop. He can't help but overhear Jacqueline Vadim say she is coming to conduct business there with Jane Somers, who was one of the midwives at Sally's head when Clarence got born.

Jane is very smart and has an hour glass figure. She stands tall as most men, and Jane has always admired stylish hats to wear. Jane is in her dressing room at the hat shop fixing her hair up so she can fit a particular hat to wear this upcoming weekend. Crash..!Boom..! Clarence rushes into the hat shop after his crash landing into the door. Jane now with her heart pounding comes panicky from her dressing room, and enters the front of the store where all of the hats are for sale.

"Miss Jane! Miss Jane!" shouts Clarence."Clarence, is that you coming in here so dumb like that?"

“Uhum...sorrry.”

“What's going on, what's wrong?"

"I just carried her bags from the train station to the hotel! And she's coming here to see you about the hats!"

"What? Who is? Whose bags did you carry from the train station?"

"She's from Paris, France and New York! Her name is Jakelll...nn... something! I don't know."

“Well now, Clarence, you're not making sense.”

“She's bringing hats for you and she is at the hotel, and now I got to go."

Jane is standing tall and erect in the middle of the room, staring at Clarence as he leaves. She is puzzled about what he was saying. After he is gone, Jane goes back to what she was doing, with all of that on her mind. And Clarence goes back to the depot. Where he finds a bearded man standing around wearing a checkered suit, and has a very stylish brim on his head. As well, he has a glass in his left eye that has a long thin chain attached. Clarence is overjoyed about the six cents he got from the French woman for carrying her bags. He is thinking of doing the same for the man in the checkered suit, so that he can get paid something from him, too.

Clarence up above moves forward at a slow walking pace, with his hand stretched out in front of him. And sliding it across the front of the depot, puzzled whether to ask if he can carry the gent's bags or not. Finally he goes over to where he is standing and greets the individual.

"Say Mr., you just got here from off the train, didn't you?" says Clarence.

"Yes that I did," the gentleman replied back to Clarence.

"And these are your bags here? I can see these are your bags," Clarence says coming forward to carry.

"Yes those are my things, what about it?"

Clarence is looking up at him as though it were to see the top of a tree. And this is Clarence's first go at it on his own. For it was the French woman first who approached him.

"Hay you there! You get away from him!"

"What! What!"

"I said stop bothering people and get out of the way!"

A deputy comes for Clarence as though a trespasser has climbed over the fence.

"That's ok, he's not bothering me," says the gent in the checkered suit.

"Well, it looks to me like he's in your way," replies the deputy.

"I wanted to see if I could carry his bags for him," Clarence speaks up, assured the gent will take his side.

"No!No!No! We have George all over the place doing that!" shouts the deputy.

"Welll... Nowww... I don't mind if the boy does."

"Yeah, jus' like I did for the lady from France. See, look, she gave me a nickel, and she gave me a penny."

Clarence has his hand wide open to show the money.

"Ok then, let's get the boy broke-in some more, and the others can just take him on as being one of the baggage carriers here at the depot," the final words coming from the gentleman, who is a doctor that comes to town on the train once in a while, to convene with the town doctor. He gets Clarence in on being a baggage carrier at the depot. The deputy had known all along whom the gentleman is, and takes a bow, then moves two steps backwards, turns about, and goes away.

3

It's almost night now and lots of excitement has filtered throughout the town. And there are visitors and business consultants, in its domains. Clarence is at the warehouse, and finds Barbo Brown stacking up crates that'll be kept there. The last of it got put up just as he arrived. So together the both of them head for home. And Clarence full of excitement is showing Barbo the money he got from the two train passengers, and as he is telling the story of how it came about, he keeps getting interrupted by Barbo, because he is excited about all of the stuff they put into the warehouse.

"Lots of stuff from the factories up North came from off the train too!" says Barbo excitedly.

"And she got to get upstairs in the good room!"

Clarence keeps talking as he makes gestures to Barbo.

"I wish I had a fist full to show you Clarence."

"Um, hu...yeah," gestures Clarence. Then he's telling Barbo some more. "And he was some dressed up man, that's whose stuff I carried the next time after the French woman."

"That's good, they're gonna have you at the depot to do that, Clarence."

And finally after a few comments from Clarence, it's the three miles from town to reach the two-room house where he was born. Clarence springs from Barbo's one-horse wagon, than sprints up the path to crash through the front door once more. He thrusts himself all the way into where his mother is lying in bed. "Moma! Mom! Its meeee..." From under the covers Clarence's mother Sally perks up and sounds off: "I know that wouldn't be you Clarence, coming in here so crazy like that. I'm in bed now because I been real busy helping Mary make dresses today. What's the matter with you anyways?" Standing at the side of the bed, he puts his hand out in front of him to show the money, saying. "See momma, look." She fades in and out of Clarence talking, but tells him to get a tin cup from the kitchen and put the money in it, then leave the tin cup on the table until the morning. He can finish telling her then.

4

"Hats from Paris, France? Oh yes... I do remember sending you a letter last year. And told of some money I have to invest."

It's the next morning and Jane's visitor comes to her hat shop. Now she understands what had Clarence so excited.

"Yes, I'm Jacqueline Vadim, the one that you'd be calling it up to."

Jacqueline is sure about the hats she brought, that they will be appropriate for the particular hat shop that Jane has in her small town. But Jacqueline did come unannounced, and wants to apologize.

"I'm sorry for not sending word directly to you here, as I did for them in New York. But you see, I wasn't sure I could come here," Jacqueline explains to the overly surprised Jane. And Jane has a look of thunder on her face, and is very much pleased at the company she's getting. That it's a French lady from Paris here by way of the New York's. She can hardly wait to tell the others. "Come in and sit down, we'll go to Joe and Betty's kitchen up the street for biscuits and tea, and talk some more there. And then come back here."

5

Clarence is waiting for Barbo to come with the wagon to take him back to the depot. He was asked to come back in the morning for cleanup. For it is always a big mess after a noonday rush of the coming of the train. Sally stops making her bed so she can take time out to talk to Clarence about last night. "That's good they're letting you be at the depot, as long as you can handle doing that," Sally continues on as she comes from the bedroom, into where the rest of the house is. "Clarence, are you sure they're letting you help out at the depot?" Sally looks down into the tin cup on the table, with the money in it. She had never known her son to lie. But cautious is Sally not to have her son sneaking around doing things he really has no business doing. "Oh yes! They're letting me mom! First the lady came and got me, and then I asked the man. Oh yeah, the lady wants Miss Jane. She's in business she has hats to sell."

"The lady that you carried the bags for?"

"Yep, and I went and told Miss Jane."

It's the late eighteen hundreds, that's getting to be the early nineteen hundreds. Clarence is considered a smart kid and to be somewhat special. Sally, well, about what her son is saying, is bewildered: "What do you mean you told Miss Jane?" Clarence tells his mother the rest of the story, and she decides to go into town when Barbo gets there as well. And just at that moment Barbo is pulling back on the reins outside in front of the house: "Woe, hold up there, kick mule! Get right their! That's good right their!" And then he's calling up to the house. "Hay up there! Are you comin' boy?"

Clarence comes running out of the house telling Barbo to wait for Sally, because she is going too. Swiftly and most excitedly, Clarence climbs aboard and is ready to start the day. And just as he gets up there, Barbo talks more about all of the goods that came in from the factories up North. He can touch bases with Clarence on what he is saying, because there are some hats in boxes that got put up as well. Finally Sally has come out of the house, and she is wearing her Sunday's best.

6

The trappers and hunters are showing off their furs, to sale or trade. And all of the markets are open and in full bloom. As well, there is wild rabbit and pheasant. And some manage to kill a deer, so venison is offered to the morning and afternoon shoppers. At Joe and Betty's, Jacqueline Vadim is showing off a couple of her best hats she brought over from Paris. "Oh that one is so pretty, and I like the feather," Jane says. All of the attention turns to their table, as though they were the life of the party. And a small crowd of women gathers around their table to be a part of the show and tell.

"Yes, yes I'll take that one," says a woman who has gathered around the table.

"And that's right, the one with the feather is so very

good," she comments.

"These are just a few to show. The rest of them are in the warehouse," says Jacqueline vadim.

"And when they get to my hat shop you can see them," says Jane.

"Well, I'll take the one that has the feather now," the woman insists.

"Its cost has not yet been decided," says Jane.

Bang! a gun blast is heard from outside. And bang again, another shot is fired: "That sounds like shoot'n," a man says aloud in the kitchen-in. And everyone on the inside quiets down and becomes motionless. They all are looking out of the big picture window at people running past, and forming a crowd where the shooting was. "What do you suppose that is?" asks another man in the kitchen-in, and pulls his wife away from Jane and Jacqueline, then goes outside.

7

Barbo has the reins held tight in his hands and Sally is sitting high upon the bunk'n-board with Clarence crimped in the middle of both of them. They can see past the driving horse, more of the long straight road. Also the clouds are not so high overhead that has the morning sun shining through. All of them put their overcoats on to protect them from the cold of the winter.

"A rider's comin' past, and he's really riding fast' too," shouts Clarence.

"We can see 'em Clarence," replies Sally.

"I wonder who it is that's coming in such a hurry," says Barbo.

He brings the horses' wagon to a halt so they can see who it is riding past so quickly.

"It's Carl Jenkins and comin' from town I'll bet," shouts Barbo. "Hay Carl, what's your hurry?" he continues.

"There's been a shoot'n in town and I'm goin' for the sheriff, he's at the sawmill," answers the fast-riding horseman without stopping. Swiftly, Barbo gets the horse and wagon continuing on its way.

8

"You people move over! Separate! Get apart!" The deputy makes his way through the crowd and looks down at the shot man lying there dead in a puddle of blood. Oooss and ahhhs come from the crowd. All of them move backwards away from the dead body and some leave the scene.

"I yelled for him to stop, but he kept on running for it!" says the deputy excitedly.

"What's it all about?" Asks a man in the crowd of people who stayed.

"He was robbing the hotel with that gun their."
A six-shot handgun is laying on the ground just ahead of the dead man.

"And I caught him red handed as I walked in. The

desk clerk had his hands held high, because of that gun on 'em. I said you their! As I was going for my gun. Along about that time he wheeled around without think'n, and took a shot at me. I ducked and moved backwards, and got back outside. I'll be dag gone if he didn't take off running past me. Well now there it is. He wouldn't stop when I said to. So, then, I took my one, then two shots. And I got'em too. Right there in back of the head. And you all here see it."

At that moment the deputy is standing-looking out at the crowd as Barbo's horse and wagon come barreling in. Now they'll find out what the shooting was all about. Just ahead they can see the crowd of people and head straight for it.

"That's got to be what was the shoot'n," says Barbo.

"Yeah, let's go see," Sally says.

When they get to the dead body the unexpected sight is with much difficulty.

"Get the boy back!" says Barbo Brown aloud to Sally.

She moves Clarence back, as well as herself. "But look who's talking to the deputy, mom? That's the man I was talking about. I carried his bags."

"Oh yes, I see 'em."

"And over there is Miss Jane with that woman. I carried her bags first."

"I see them too, let's go over there."

Within an instant Clarence and his mother get to

Jane Somers, and she has Jacqueline Vadim with her. It is like a celebration, just then. However, what invites them all there is no celebration.

"I can understand you shoot'n ‘em deputy Barns."

"Yes, Doctor Quake, that's right. And Doctor I'm wondering where he comes from. I've never seen him in town before," finishes deputy Barns.

“He don't come from nowhere, no Sir, nowhere at all. Do you see them boots he’s wearing?" Doctor Quake asks.

"Yeah, I see ‘em." answers Deputy Barns.

"They're boots of two different kinds," says Doctor Quake.

"That's right, their not a pair,” the Deputy again.

"And, as for the rest of it, them trousers don't fit ‘em, and that coat don't no ways belong to him, neither," says Doctor Quake.

"I see, so he's just rambling around with no where's to go?"

"That's right, Deputy Barns, stole away on the train, and gets himself a horse any ole kind of way, probably too.”

By the time the sheriff got there, Doctor Quake and Deputy Barns have already taken the body to the morgue. And the crowd disperses.

9

A few weeks have passed by after the shooting, and Jacqueline Vadim has come and gone. Jane manages to get the hat shop filled up with hats and has been very busy. Mr. Foster has work for Clarence at the depot almost every day now. Rather a train is there or not.

"Good morning Mr. Foster," says Clarence.

"Good morning Clarence. I see you made it in ok."

"Yes, I did."

"Well, since you did. Go and get your employee timetable from off my desk, and I'll getcha started."

There's very little talking after that, for they all are busy with their daily routine. And all's quiet throughout the small Virginia town. For lunch, Clarence has a tuna fish sandwich and an apple. He takes a quart jar to the well nearby and fills it with water for something to drink.

In times passing, it's another time a stack's puff, puff, puffing is rolling over the railroad tracks and hard driven coming into the train yard. The train has all cargo and no people. Standing by is Barbo Brown, he is waiting patiently to offload the cargo. And Clarence comes outside of the depot to help Barbo along with the others. Clarence is a grown man now and is able to provide for himself. The train stops, and the men are opening the big boxcar doors. It's a shipment full of stuff from the Northern part of the country. It came from Ohio, Michigan, and Wisconsin. Barbo climbs up into the boxcar. "Heads up, here it comes," he shouts, then slides a crate to the open door for Clarence to reach up and get. "Wow!" This is too heavy," Clarence immediately puts the heavy crate down on the ground. Barbo is quick to examine the next crate before he gives it to Clarence. "Well, no wonder it's heavy. These are full of metal things for the hardware store. This crate has door hinges. And this one is full of nails," Barbo continues. "Then you had best double up with one of the others, Clarence," finishes Barbo. Clarence does and can continue with the off loading of the train.

10

Jane Somers is very prosperous at the hat shop. With open doors she invites her townspeople in, so they can shop for a new hat to wear. It is a good and prosperous town to the individual. He or she can walk around with their head up high and smiling nice. The streets now have automobiles, as well as some horses.

Barnstorming is overhead, and at a fast moving pace lots of people are gathering around to watch the acrobat on the airplane. He is out of the airplane on one wing standing on his head. And tossing himself about, as the airplane flies high up in the sky. The crowd below is applauding at the Barnstorming. "That's some acrobat ain't it?!" Mary arises from out of the domains of the crowd, and screams it over top of all the people.

"Yes, that is something," answers Sally.

"But you don't have to scream at us about it, Mary. We're standing here next to you," replies Jane.

The plane lands nearby, out in the clear. "Oh good, we get to see 'em," Mary again. This time she does keep her voice down even though she is still excited. And the crowd goes over to greet the pilot and the acrobat. Clarence doesn't get to see the Barnstorming because he went fishing instead of coming into town.

Sally wants to move from the small house on the outskirts, to one of the neighborhood houses in town. She wants to remarry and can see more people living in town. It's been long enough now, after the death of her husband, Clarence senior. She would like to confide in another man who is suitable for her and her son. More years have come and gone. Clarence has a steady income at the depot, and what his mother could produce did get them moved out of the country side and into town. But there was no money saved in the tin cup, because Clarence spent it. As well Sally did get to know a man named Nathaniel Williams who is called Nate. Moreover, they are considering their moments of matrimony. The threesome is adults footing the bill, as long as they're living in the same house. And Sally's husband Nate is a good lover. And her woman femininity has it as being in good company with her companion's masculine physique.

Part Two

Going North

11

"Let's not go on about it anymore Clarence. It's because of black Thursday and black Tuesday, in 1929. That's how come we have this. And the trains go where the money is."

"Ok Mr. Foster, I understand that. But they do say in Toledo Ohio the factories are still going on and it's possible to get work."

"Yes, that's right, Clarence. The Ford Automobile and other companies are still at it."

“Since you have to let me go here at the depot, I'm thinking of going to Toledo."

"Yes, but how will you get there?"

"I'm thinking of taking a passenger train sometime out of here."

"Well, if you got enough money saved up, for even after you get there, then go ahead."

Mr. Foster pays Clarence Taylor his final pay, and bids him farewell.

Clarence comes back to look at the schedule, to see when a passenger train will be coming. For it is twoyears later after the great stock market crash, and as it stands here in 1931, they are unable to keep their jobs and have a good economy in their town. So he decides to leave and is going to Toledo, Ohio. Because of all the great stories about a factory worker who makes ends meet.

"Hello Clarence, what brings you around by our way today?" asks one of the depot attendants who still has his job.

"I want to know if I can take a passenger train to Ohio this month, because I'm going to work at a factory in Toledo."

"Oh, well, my goodness. I can tell you now, it'll be in two weeks on Friday, hopefully. As long as they don't switch tracks on us again, or if a train doesn't get derailed," continues the attendant.

"Ok, I'll check back then," says Clarence.

He decides to walk home after leaving the depot, and he is taking a short cut through the park. Some people are standing around vagrant; they have no house to go home to. Also there are men sitting on park benches mumbling to themselves. Clarence is walking as quickly as he can, and he is trying not to notice.

“Here's the last bit of food we have left. There'll be supper today but I don't know about tomorrow," Sally says to Nate with the kitchen cabinet doors wide open.

"Ok Sally," says Nate.

“Clarence worked the whole week at the depot when he got his final pay," Sally continues on.

"Maybe he'll still have something when he comes in," she finishes.

"Yeah, maybe," answers Nate.

Quick hops up the front porch steps, then onto the porch and through the front door comes Clarence with all of his final pay.

"Clarence is that you, that just came in?" asks Sally.

"Yes, it's me," answers Clarence.

"We're out here in the kitchen, and we were just talking about you. Come here and sit down,” Sally says.

Before Clarence can tell his mother and Nate what he plans to do, they explain the situation. He doesn’t say anything and gives them better than half his money. Clarence has always lived at home with his mother. It was not too difficult because of it only being the two of them. Sally and Nate are an older couple who appreciate someone around to help out with things. Clarence wants to get married and have children someday. Because he is an only child, he really fills to.

His girlfriend's name is Norma. She and Clarence know each other from the outskirts of town, where the both of them have grown up. Norma is with high check bones and brown button eyes. Her hair is reddish brown and shoulder length. She stands five feet tall and has bronzy brown skin. Norma is very pretty and has a positive mental attitude. They hardly say a word at the supper table. And Sally has decided to go for more food at the grocery store tomorrow. Its night now and Clarence is lying in bed with his eyes open and looking up at the ceiling. He is thinking of the train ride to Toledo and what it must be like to work at a factory once he gets there. Thoughts of getting paid money enter into his mind. And living in a house that has the Toledo people for neighbors, and getting the outings that they do. As well he thinks of sending money back to his mother and her husband Nate. His eyes have become too heavy to keep open. Restless on his back, Clarence turns over on one side, then goes to sleep.

12

After the harvest, this time of the year brings about a very colorful outdoors. The leaves are changing color on the trees, and the air is filled with the smell of a wooded forest. There are a lot of people moving about to see what they can do and gain in their lives. These are the hungry years. Some have a sign posted: apple five cents. They got them from the shipping and receiving warehouse in their town. And it's been a few days into the two weeks that Clarence anticipates leaving. Still he is used to the routine of going to work at the depot. After having strolled through the park, Clarence enters into the downtown area and makes his way to the depot. He doesn't stop to talk to anyone before he reaches the door. Once inside, he can see Mr. Foster.

"Well hello Clarence! Did you stop in for a visit, and to talk awhile?" asks Mr. Foster.

"Yes, that, and to see if I can get some work for a couple of days or something."

"No, it's still too slow. And it's only been a few days since I had to let you go. But sit anyways."

Clarence does sit awhile and talks to Mr. Foster. And then he walks around town some to see what he can get himself into. Still there's nothing much to speak of, except the poor living conditions. A thing to do, though, has always been going fishing. But it's the wrong time of the day to go, because the fish are not biting. So he plans to go to the river first thing in the morning.

Strolling along, Clarence can't help but think of Toledo, and he has become very eager to go. By the time he reaches home, rain is falling. Nevertheless, Clarence picks-up the pace and keeps walking. His mother Sally has a large pot of cabbage stew on the stove, and butter and bread on the table. She's in the kitchen stirring the pot of cabbage stew and wishing for someone to talk to. Nate has gone out for the day, so she is home alone.

In steps Clarence and he is very wet from getting caught out in the rain. "I can always tell when you come in, Clarence. Because you come crashing through the door as if you're breaking in," Sally says as she comes from the kitchen into the living room.

"I'm hurrying up get 'n out of the rain, mom."

"It looks as though it's too late for that. But I can see

it's raining hard from the kitchen windows."

"I know it, is Nate here? There's something I want to tell you."

"No, Nate's out for the day. He's trying to get work. What do you have to tell us?"

"I plan to leave."

"Leave for where...when?"

His mind races for a moment before he can tell her, because it is a nervy thing to do. Then Clarence talks of the goings on in their town. And he is looking another way. He explains working at a factory in Toledo, Ohio. But little do they know is, better than half the people are out of work in Toledo. As well Ford Motor Company cut its payroll back the biggest ever.

"Nate's gonna be surprised to hear it when he comes in tonight," Sally says.

"I know, mom. I wanted to tell you before, but I just didn't say anything," says Clarence.

"I see, but you remember to tell Nate when he gets in."

"Ok, I'll tell 'em."

The rain has stopped and it's the end of the day. Nate has just come home and he couldn't get any work for the day, or a job to start later on. Sally and Clarence are sitting in the living room. They've already eaten and Sally rises from the sofa and is escorting Nate to the kitchen so he can eat too. He washes his face and hands in the sink and then sits down at the supper table. Before Sally can bring the cabbage stew from the pot to his plate, it needs to be reheated. After lighting the stove she turns to Nate and is telling him what Clarence's intentions are. And just into the conversation Nate is calling for Clarence to come into the kitchen.

"What's going on Clarence, your mother's saying something about you getting out of here?"

"I'm going up North to Toledo, Ohio so I can work in a factory up there."

"Oh, I don't know. Things are bad all over the country to me. You should look into it more first," Nate finishes.

"Well, you see, I heard talk of it at the depot. When I was working there. It's a lot to do with supplies coming from industries," answers Clarence.

"Yes, that's true. But you see, something's going on now that could have all of that changed out not so good," says Nate.

They talk about it a bit more, with Nate at the supper table.

Then Clarence gets up from the table and leaves them there in the kitchen. He goes up the stairs to his bedroom where he does his thinking most. But there's a knock at the door. And it's Clarence's girlfriend Norma Johnson. She usually has Clarence over to her house, rather then see him there. However, his head just now hit the pillow and Sally is calling up to him. Quick dressed and dashing down the stairs, he sees Norma getting comfortable on the sofa.

"Are you in bed Clarence?" asks Norma.

"Not really, I was gonna do me some thinkin'. It's good to see you, and I'm glad you came over," says Clarence.

"I got to missing you because I haven't seen you for a few days, so I thought I'd come over and see what's up," says Norma.

"Well, I plan to go fishing at the river tomorrow morning and then I was going to see you. There is something I want to tell you Norma."

"Hopefully it'll be some good news, because I'm over do for that."

Clarence takes no time telling his feelings on the matter of being out of work, and he can no longer stand it there at home in their town. So he's going away to Toledo. She tells him to take more time as Nate suggested, to be better prepared. And with all of that on her mind, Norma leaves for home. Then Clarence climbs the stairs one last time that night.

Cool is the night because of the rainfall earlier. And Norma in her Ford automobile just stops cold in the street. She'd been experiencing car trouble and finally it has shut down completely. She manages to push the car from the middle of the street off to the side. And her house is closer to walk, rather than go back to Clarence's. But she still has a long walk, and the fall of the year night is cold next to winter. Norma had put on a sweater for warmth earlier that day, and nothing more. With long and fast stepping strides she swiftly walks down the street. And the street is still wet and has water puddles. There is no paved sidewalk along the side. As well, no other drivers have happened by to pick her up. It's dark without streetlights and there are no houses along the way at this point, because she lives out of town in the country.

At dawn of the morning sun, Clarence is still under the covers and fast asleep. A loud bang from a car backfiring outside awakens him. Clarence sits up in bed. Then he puts his feet down on the floor and remains seated on the bed. He takes a few minutes to clear his head and then springs up and out of bed. And he is first to roam the house this morning. After a quick breakfast to start the day, Clarence gets outside with his fishing pole, extra tackle, and a can of worms. He considers that going fishing wouldn't be any good this time as well, because it rained yesterday. And the river would be too muddy. But he has it on his mind to go for activity, so he goes.

13

There was no fire lighted in the pot belly wood-burning stove, when Norma got to her house in the A.M. And now the sun is up and she is lying in bed shivering from being overly exposed to the after midnight cold. Her feelings of discomfort have her awake and not awake. She is lying on her stomach, then back on one side again. Three houses up the road is where her mother lives, and her sister. Unlike Clarence, Norma has a house of her own. She managed to get it because of her Uncle. He built the house for his own place of residence. He moved to North Carolina after having married one of its native women and gave the house to Norma. A sneeze and then sneezing again. She's quick up and thrust out of bed to go wipe her nose and to clear her stuffy head. Norma's sister Martha is at the front door twisting and turning the knob to get in. The door is locked, so she is tapping on the window. Norma comes from the bathroom to the front dressed in her nightgown. She pulls the blind to one side. Looking out of the window, she can see Martha there on the front porch. Like always, Martha came over to sit with Norma and talk a while. As Martha comes through the door she can see that something is wrong with her sister.

"You sure are looking bad this morning-wiping your nose with them tissues," says Martha after entering and closing the door.

"I know it. My car broke down last knight just outside of town after I left Clarence. And it wouldn't start up again."

“It did? What did you do?"

"I had to walk it. And it was so very cold last night. And now I'm coming down with this bad cold."

"Mom's got something at the house for that. I'll go get it in a minute. You said, you had to walk it?" finishes Martha.

"Yes, after I pushed the car to the side of the road," answers Norma.

"Just how far away were you?" asks Martha.

"I was out of town coming here. And it was too far to walk back the other way. It took me from after eleven o'clock last night, until the wee hours this morning to get home."

"Yeah, but it's still getting warm enough at daytime

not to have a fire in your stove. And look outside at the sun coming up good this morning. Because it's gonna be a warm day," finishes Martha.

They can see out of the living room windows, a heated sun is already brilliant in the sky. And the morning's glow has its warmth everywhere. Martha leaves her sister's house to tell the others what happened, and to get the concoction their mother has for a cold. And Norma decides not to have a fire in the stove, but to wait it out.

14

A large carp stirs up the water splashing and swirling, fighting its way off Clarence's hook. His bamboo king pole is stretched out across the water at a calm place of the rivers run. Dipping deep down into the water and tugging at the line, the big fish is putting up its biggest fight. But within moments Clarence has the fish to the surface because it has grown too tired to keep fighting. And he manages to get it ashore where he is standing. "Hay you there!" A man has just sounded off at Clarence. He is standing above on higher ground. "What ya gonna do with that fish?" he asks.

"Umm...I'm trying to catch some and take'em home. So I'm gonna keep it," answers Clarence.

"Sure, but you can let me have that one since you

can catch more," he's walking down to where Clarence is, and has a long stick with a bundle tied to it. His clothes are old and worn, as well they've been stitched together in places, and there are patches all over. All of which is to a rambling Hobo. The startled Clarence, who's turned to the voice coming towards him, now, has the carp gripped in his hands. And the bamboo king pole that has a string, bobber, and hook, attached to it rests at his feet.

"I never seen you around here before. Who are you?" asks Clarence.

"You could say I'm something of a traveler! Got here in your town sometime ago. From off the train! Been camping out up there along the river with the rest of 'em. And I ain't got nothin' to fish with or else I'd catch'em myself. Have you got some extra tackle, so I can make me up something?"

"Yelll...wait a minute. Let me get'em on my stringer and put 'em back down in the water to keep 'em. I got some extra tackle in that bag. In case I get hung up on a snag, you can have some of that," answers Clarence.

"Ok."

After Clarence finishes putting the carp on the stringer and into the water, he gets the extra fishing tackle and puts it at the Hobo's feet.

"I'll find me a stick suitable for a fishing pole now," he says.

"Where did you say you were from?" asks Clarence.

"I didn't! Came in on a train, and from traveling all

over. Because of what's hit‘n. But you people ain't got no nothing either. So...then, as soon as the next train arrives I'm get ‘n on it," says the Hobo.

"What ya mean, what are you talking about?" asks Clarence.

The Hobo manages to find a long stick on the ground nearby to use for a fishing pole. He gets a worm from out of the can and is explaining to Clarence.

"Hopping trains is what it is," he says, as he puts a night crawler on the hook, "And in most cases you go where it takes ya. Because they can't keep to the schedule anymore," finishes the Hobo.

"Hopping trains-that’s dangerous. I plan to go to Toledo, Ohio and get work at a factory. But we don't know if we're going to get a passenger train on schedule or not," says Clarence.

"You mean the one that's due in next week?" asks the Hobo.

"Yes, at noon on Friday," answers Clarence.

"Hay wait a minute. You said passenger train on Friday," replies the Hobo.

"That's right," answers Clarence.

"Oh no, that's when you pay money to ride. I mean the one coming in before. That's due in Wednesday," finishes the Hobo.

"Wednesday train ain't no passenger train. It'll be hauling cargo,” says Clarence.

"Yeah, so you don't say? What ya do is just get on

board and make sure no one can see ya when you do. Especially one of the bulls, or the shacks. The bulls are private police hired by the railroad, and the shacks are the railroad crew," says the Hobo as he tosses the baited hook into the river. The hobo is explaining to Clarence how to hop trains. But Clarence use to work at the depot, so he knows what the bulls and shacks are. The carp and some catfish are the catch from the muddy murky water for the day.

Down river from where Clarence and the Hobo are fishing, there are people living in something they built out of scrap sheet metal and wooden packing boxes. Some have pitched a tent. President Herbert Hoover refused aid to poor people because he felt that matter is for state's governors and charity organizations to do. But they too are without money. People thought progression was going to happen quickly with Hoover as President. But it just lingered on.

"I can't believe the way people are living near the river. We've never been this way before," says Clarence.

"That's Hooverville people," answers the Hobo.

"Hoovervilles?" replies Clarence.

"Yeah, Hoovervilles. After the President Herbert Hoover. He still ain't made things right yet. People living in shacks like that are getting to the outside of big towns and flopping there," explains the Hobo.

He finishes telling Clarence and both of them have caught their final catch of the day, and have gone each own way.

15

Here in the small Virginian town, Nate Williams had worked as a hired hand for almost everything there was to do. And now that is no means of support. He is sitting at the supper table with a plate of beans in front of him. After being out in town looking for work, again, he's talking to Sally about the way things are since the great stock market crash. He too couldn't help but notice people homeless and in a very bad way.

"Sally you know it's a darn shame what's goin' on. I still can't find any work," says Nate.

"I know, and that goes for a lot of people around here in their homes too," replies Sally.

"That's right, and if it keeps up, all of us are gonna be out there on our butts jus' like I been seeing it,says Nate.

"I can see Clarence coming through the back alley. And he caught some fish. That's where he's been, he went fishing today," Sally says.

"Good, I'm glad he found something to do with his time," says Nate.

Clarence indeed did come through the back alleyway for home. And he is putting his fishing gear in a shed before entering into the house. Then he goes in with a stringer of fish.

"Hi Clarence, you did all right on that fish bank I can see," Sally says.

"Yep, I caught these carp and catfish," he answers.

"That's good Clarence, go ahead and put them over there in the sink and I'll help you fix 'em up here in a minute," says Nate.

"Well...here, Clarence, I'll get you a plate too, and you can join Nate sitting there at the table." Sally gets a plate from the kitchen cabinet and heaps two big ladles full down on it. And then puts the hot steaming plate of bean soup down on the table across from Nate. The catch of the day is in the kitchen sink filled with water. Sally puts two slices of bread on a saucer for Clarence as well. There is butter on the table. The carp and catfish are steering up water in the sink, and the splashing and swirling about gets water down on the floor. Sally comes with a mop, to mop up the spill. Then she puts her hand almost at arm's length down into the fishy water to open the stopper and bring it to a lower level.

"Are you still thinking about leaving Clarence?" asks Nate.

"Yes, I am. And someone came up to me today when I was fishing. He wanted to fish too. So I gave him some of my fishing tackle. He's from all over, he said. And came here on a train," says Clarence.

"What all did he have to say Clarence?" Sally chimes in.

Clarence tells them the talking that he and the Hobo had about the Hoovervilles and what it is to President Herbert Hoover. And he talked about the people living down at the riverside. But Clarence says nothing about hopping trains. Because he's thinking of doing just that to get to Toledo Ohio, and there's no getting them to understand that. The next day Clarence goes to Norma's house and she is telling him what happened on the night she left his house and had to walk because of her car breaking down. Norma developed a cough she can't control, and it's taking her over. Her sister Martha is there too. They're all in the living room zealous about Norma's condition. Norma complains, the concoction her mother made doesn't work. But she is taking it anyway. "I'm gonna have ta find you something else since that doesn't work," says Martha.

"It's only been a few days, I'll give it some more time. Leave me and Clarence alone for now Martha. Because I want to talk to him," says Norma as she's trying to keep from coughing and sneezing.

"Ok, I'll see you later."

Martha leaves and Norma tells Clarence to come sit next to her on the sofa. He climbs out of a big chair across the room, and puts his arms around Norma, then pulls her close to him when he gets there. She is still dressed in her night clothes and has on a robe. She is sitting at the very end of the sofa with her legs and feet curled underneath her rump and in Clarence's arms. There is a cup of tea on the end table as well as the concoction.

"I'm wondering how you feel about us. Because we've been together for a long time now and you still don't want to get married," she says.

"Oh that's what it is. This is why you asked Martha to leave and it's just the two of us."

"Yes, I want to know how you feel, and what's going on that you're leaving for Toledo?"

"Well...you know I don't have my job at the depot no more. So there's no money. And look at how it is these days."

"We can live here in my house."

"Still there wouldn't be any money."

A series of coughs and a couple of sneezes causes Norma to pull away from Clarence. She brings her legs and feet from underneath her rump then puts her head in her lap and her feet flat on the floor. Clarence, trying to soothe her puts his hand on her back and in a circular motion moves it about for a good sensation. Norma is reaching for the concoction that will soothe her throat, but it isn't the cure. She is able to collect herself in a few minutes. With squinty teary eyes, she looks over at Clarence. She is telling him to help her to bed so she can lie down. He helps her to it, and lights a fire in the wood-burning stove.

16

The nights are very cold now and the leaves on the trees have turned color, and are falling to the ground. One depot attendant comes down the stairs from up in the lookout tower that's to the depot. He is looking to see if he can see a train coming from far away. And there is nothing. Not the cargo train two days before or the passenger train. Clarence is at the depot sitting in a chair near the lighted fireplace. There is one log burning in the fireplace. Tall orange and red flames climb up into the chimney. The attendant from the lookout tower has entered into the room with a look of disgust on his face.

"There's not going to be a train. It's been long enough to wait and again I have walked the stairs up to the lookout tower. Its well into the evening now, what was due in at noon ain't coming. So people, stay if you want to, or head for home," he concludes.

The warmth from the fire has everybody seated calmly in their seats. Some people are standing. There are some oosss...and ohhhhs...with the sighing after he talks. Then they're quiet again.

As they all sit thoughtless to themselves, a fight breaks out in the town store not far from the depot. "Go for the sheriff and get the deputy, as I hold 'em here," shouts the store clerk at a lady who's shopping in the store. She dashes out empty handed as fast as a lady can go. And within seconds she gets to the sheriff's office across the street, and down one block. Deputy Barns is sitting at his desk near the front door with a cup of coffee in his hands. Boom! Into the sheriffs office she goes crazed and as though on fire.

"Is that you sit'n their deputy Barns?"

"That's right! What is it?"

"It's at the store over across the street, Macks Market. He caught some out of Towner trying to steal money from the cashier drawer on the counter. And he's got 'em held there right now. Bring the Sheriff too!"

"The sheriff is out, so you move out of the way now and let's just get me over there!" From out of the sheriff's office they come hurriedly.

The thief and store clerk are still in a tussle inside. A big forearm comes down on the clerk, which causes him to let go and drop on one knee. At that instant the thief heads for the door. The clerk lunges after him with one hand reaching, slaps the heel of his foot, causing the thief to trip some. But he still gets to the door and outside, staggering. The front door of the store remains open and the clerk can see the deputy getting across the street well ahead of the lady.

"That's him right their going! Didn't you see ‘em just get out of here deputy Barns? You get ‘em!” shouts the store clerk as he too is coming for the door.

"I see ‘em! You stop right there!" The deputy sounds off at the thief and withdraws his revolver from the holster. But the thief takes off running, to cross the street just ahead of deputy Barns instead of stopping. "You people get out of the way!” The deputy shouts once more and everybody on the other side drops. He fires two shots right off and misses, but shoots the thief with the next shot fired and kills him. The bullet penetrated the side of the thief, piercing his heart, rather than get him in back of the head. Deputy Barns goes quickly to the dead man so he can see who it is. People are spilling out of the downtown places and into the street, gathering around the shooting.

From out of the depot comes Clarence Taylor and all of the rest of them to see what happened after they heard the gunshots fired. "Don't get too close people! Stand back a ways!” commands the deputy. But people still are running to see and getting close. Clarence makes his way to the front of the crowd and is looking down at the dead man.

"Who is it?" asks one in the crowd.

"I don't know, I can't get a good look at ’em," says

another. “Let's go around this way, maybe we can see from over there."

The deputy trying to control the crowd can't help his eyes but see the individual laying there dead.

"That's who I was talking to when I was fishing last week," Clarence, devastated, speaks up to the deputy. Then Deputy Barns looks over at Clarence who's across from him very seriously, and all of a sudden all's quiet.

"You can identify him?" asks Deputy Barns.

"Yes, that's right. I was fishing at the river and he saw me and wanted to catch some fish too. So I gave him some of my fishing tackle," Clarence explains.

"Did he tell you his name or where he's from?" asks the deputy, convulsed and with all of his attention at Clarence.

"He didn't say what his name was. Only that he's hopping trains and comes from all over!" answers Clarence.

"Yeah...that's a hobo alright. To hear that and see ‘em there," says Deputy Barns.

"Did he speak on any place in particular where he was staying around here?" he continues.

"Yes, he told me that he was camping out down by the river where the others are. Maybe you can ask some questions there," answers Clarence.

After the deputy and Clarence discuss that back and forth, Clarence goes back into the crowd and leaves for home. So do a lot of other people in the crowd, but still some remain to watch the dead body get carried off to the morgue. The buildings are made of brick and are two or three stories high, with some streets of brick and paved sidewalks. There isn't a cloud in the sky on the day of the shooting.

A train finally does come a few days later, at night. However, Clarence is nowhere around when it gets there. But he is still determined to make it to Toledo. So he is holding on to the few dollars left from his final pay at the depot.

17

Breathing heavily, and steadfast in the bed now is Norma. She has become very sick. Her sister Martha and mother are there and have considered going for the doctor.

"No, don't go for him because we'll have to give him something for looking in on me and we don't have it," says Norma.

"But your eyes are red. And you're so feverish," her mother says.

"Yeah...you look bad," says Martha.

"Yes, I know. Let me have a few more days this week, and we'll see."

Norma talks just above a whisper, as though she was too drowsy to open her mouth and speak. And a tea-pot full of brewed tea sits upon the burner of the kitchen stove.

No one else comes to Norma Johnson's house that day. Not Clarence, nor do they go for the doctor.

Love comes into Clarence as he's sitting at home in the big easy chair in the living room, looking out of the window. He is thinking of Norma and the times they had. He now realizes she is the very special one to marry, and have the life it is to be. He gets up from the chair and goes over to the window. His feelings are overwhelmed with passion and have his imagination running wild. Looking out of the window, Clarence can see the very colorful fall of the year's leaves blowing in the wind. The trees are becoming more and more stick-like and tall in the sky. He thinks to himself, winter is almost here now. He has become emotional longing for his woman in the cold and lonely nights.

There were two automobiles bought-used, at Clarence's house. They lasted for only a while as Norma's did. So Clarence has to ask a neighbor for a ride. But will not impose, upon them because of the way things are. The day is a bit gloomy, without any sunshine, which brings the dark about quickly. And in the dark there are fires burning in trash barrels for warmth, for those who are outside and can't get indoors. Down at the riverside, logs are used to make a campfire. There is a large kettle full of beef stew cooked over the fire. That is the fixings for the people there. A large ladle dips deep down into the kettle of beef stew and fills the tin plates. One with his guitar sits on the ground off from all of the others and rests his back against a tree. His guitar is gripped in one hand, with long skinny fingers laid to the strings, and strumming with the other hand. He's singing a folksong and some others go over to where he is to listen and sing to.

18

Norma becomes even more ill, so Martha goes for the doctor, and it is no good after he gets there.

"Well, that's all I can do for now," says the doctor,

"How long before she's better?" asks Martha.

"I told you its pneumonia. And it depends on how much bacteria there are to that fluid down in the lungs."

Their mother sits quietly and sad on the edge of the bed by Norma's side. She is 1ooking into her daughter's face, not knowing what to say. Nevertheless, she will be there for her to do whatever she can.

"Made-up old remedies won't do it any good. Keep giving her juice as cool as you can get it, and that'll help with the fever. Keep her resting in bed."

"Are you sure it's as bad as all of that doctor?" asks Martha.

"Inflammation of lung tissue is present. And the breathing of a person with pneumonia makes that sound. The fever she has with those chills and coughs, I'm sure."

He puts his stethoscope and other medical supplies back into his bag and leaves.

Norma's mother, still sitting there at Norma's side, pulls the covers over Norma's shoulders. Then she goes into the living room where Martha is.

"She don't look good mom," says Martha.

"No, but she's asleep now, and maybe it'll be better in the morning, since the doctor been here."

"But he couldn't do anything for it."

“Maybe she'll get better rest and it'll pass."

The both of them decide to spend the night there because of Norma's condition. They put their bedtime clothes on. Martha gets on the sofa, and their mother goes into the spare bedroom.

19

Nate Williams manages to get some work. He gets paid the minimum wage of twenty-five cents an hour, but doesn't work a full week. And he won't let Sally work, because he feels a woman's place is in the home. He knows the antagonism she would get from men in the workplace, and what other wives would say who are still in the home and not working. Also, the mistaken belief that women were taking jobs from men is the reason for Sally not working. But Clarence works the same as Nate. And for him too, the days worked are not enough to amount to anything. And the work is very hard labor-it's hardly worth the money. So Clarence is still looking forward to Toledo. Clarence, his mother Sally and Nate, are all settled in the house for the evening, and have eaten their supper.

Family problems come up because of their empty wallets and pocket book. It's as though all of the pleasures are taken out of life. Nate had never used any money for buying booze, which would be even more detrimental to their relationship. But still, the role model a man is in the home diminishes, because he is not the big provider anymore. Low self-esteem and not enough work or money makes everything worse. At first Sally tries to encourage her man. But as bad feelings grow from sitting around, she brings up faults in her husband. They say things not so good to each other, things they've never said before.

There is knocking at the front door of Clarence Taylor's house. Sally comes from the kitchen for the door, as Clarence does from upstairs. "I'll get it Clarence," she says looking up at him as she's going past. He then goes swiftly back to his bedroom. Sally opens the door to her neighbor from across the street. She is a young woman of twenty who comes over from time to time to talk with Sally.

"Oh, hi Gretchen, come in," Sally says.

"Ok."

"What's going on, are you just coming over to sit awhile?"

"I'm glad you asked me that because something happened, and I'm just gonna tell it to ya," Gretchen says with sad eyes at Sally and sobbing as she steps inside.

"We got a phone call just now and it was Martha Johnson. Clarence's girlfriend Norma's sister, she continues.

"Boy, from the looks of you, it wasn't good that she called," replies Sally.

"Welll...you know Norma took sick awhile back there, and they eventually went for the doctor. He said she had pneumonia, and he couldn't do anything. And now she's dead. Martha said on the telephone she must have died last night in her sleep from it."

"Oh my goodness. Let me call to Clarence, he's upstairs."

When Clarence goes downstairs and is told Norma died, he changes instantly into a weeping little boy, and crimped over holding himself.

A large funeral takes place to put Norma to rest. And all of her friends and family mourn to it's utmost as does Clarence.

The small Virginian town has become functionless, and everyone is getting eager for something good to come about. But Clarence has given up on his town; he needs to make a change. And Norma is dead. The money he had kept back is just about spent. And it's getting too cold to head north now. There is nothing for Clarence, and he can see the dead weight he'll be at home. He is thinking out of desperation and wants to leave for Toledo in spite of the cold. Thoughts of what the hobo told him about hopping trains before he was gunned down by the deputy enter into his mind. He thinks about running alongside of a train after it leaves the depot, and coming out of the brush for it. And it'll be going slow enough then. Again Clarence finds himself alone upstairs of his mother's house lying in a bed that has always been his own. He also can't help but think of Norma and the way she died of pneumonia. It seemed because she got overly exposed to the outdoors, and he don't want that to happen to him. Clarence is thinking though maybe, just maybe, he'll keep warm in a boxcar if he gets aboard. With that thought he is able to find confidence enough to go, than stay and burden his people.

20

At the hat shop Jane Somers is putting another slash through the price of the hats. They have been marked down three quarters, rather than half of the going rate. A gentleman has entered into the hat shop from off the street. "Well hello there," says Jane. He acknowledge her with a friendly gesture, saying. "Hi" and presses on more forward, to the burning hot pot belly stove, filled with hot burning coal, where the far wall from the door is. Then he extends his arms and hands out in front of him, rubbing his hands together to warm up. And with a chuckling face, he looks over his shoulder at Jane Somers. With beguiling sorrow to come in and get warm he says. "Hi, I'm Charles Benson. Do you remember me? I grew up on the East side of town. And used to work with the farmers and the fur-traders, when fur-trading was good this time of the year."

"Did you come in to buy a hat, as well as get warm Charles Benson?"

"No, I can't because I ain't got it. And I can't stay at my house no more because I ain't got that, either. That's how come I'm in here."

"Ok, but you'll have to leave. I can't stand it when everybody tries to come in for warmth, and don't buy a hat."

"Well, let me get warmed up now that I'm here, then I'll go. But you do remember me, don't you? I used to come past here all the time. I'm from near here."

"Yes, I can remember your face coming and going out there. But still, you'll have to go. Because I can't have people barging in on me and hanging around, because I haven't got it either." Charles Benson says "Ok" softly and pleasant. Then he turns away from the stove and walks out of Jane Somers' hat shop. There is a soup kitchen at the church where Haddy and Mary are. They're helping with the food servicing line, and people are standing in a long line from inside all the way out on the sidewalk, and then headed down the street and around the corner. There are two very large kettles of soup to offer. One has navy beans, and the other is full of vegetable soup.

21

Finally a train does come carrying cargo rather than a train full of passengers. And from out of the domains of the wooded forest and into the troubled little Virginian Town it goes. With the steaming engine at its front, onward to the depot. The noonday train itself can hardly wait to shut down and get serviced. For it has come from far off. And gathered there at the depot is Barbo along with a few other individuals, all of whom are keeping watch just in case a train does come in on schedule, as this cargo train did. And now at its final approach. All of the breaks are applied and the train comes to a screeching halt. From out of the lookout tower comes the telegraph operator and joins in with the others.

"Well, hello there! It's good to see that you made it!" shouts Barbo with glee.

"Yeah, we're here! How goes it with you people?"

The conductor shouts back as he comes towards the lot of them standing there.

"It's not so good. The supplies all ran out and everyone's scrounging up whatever they can get," says the telegraph operator.

"That's it all over. And we can't help but leave only so much," says the conductor.

"Yeah...we know it, and I got the message that you'll get here when you did. So here are some of us. And if we need more people to help out, we can go and fetch 'em," finishes the telegraph operator.

When the train comes through town it can't help but to be seen by a lot of the others. So a crowd forms up, and the word goes all over town like wildfire, that a train is in town. Clarence, who got told, comes at once. And he is excited to see the giant locomotive there with its freight cars. He manages to get through the crowd, then slips in and hears the Engineer and a breakeman talking about the mission of the train to those inside the depot. It's just the very talking he wanted to hear. The train will be headed north to Ohio. But it'll be going to Cincinnati and not Toledo. Clarence plans to leave in the morning and get aboard as the Hobo would. And then he can pay the fare that's to a passenger train from Cincinnati to Toledo. The men hard at work are unloading the cargo from out of freight cars, and stow it into a nearby warehouse.

Clarence doesn't get to help Barbo and the others this time. So he goes home and is upstairs in his bedroom. He can remember the hobo's satchel on the fish bank at the river, and the way his things were fixed up in it, tied to a stick. Clarence manages to make something up in a bundle like that. It's without a big stick though. Clarence puts the bundle down on the floor at the foot of his bed. And then he strips down to his T-shirt and boxing shorts. He climbs into bed and rolls over on his back looking up at the ceiling-thinking as he always has.

Leaving tomorrow morning is going to be a dream comes true. Because there'll be better living conditions and work. Also he's thinking of how grand it will be, getting to know some other people. Little does he know that it is hungry everywhere. The night lingers on, and insomnia has Clarence with eyes wide open, as though he were a young lad waiting to open Christmas presents on Christmas morning.

22

The engineer is sitting at the helm as the locomotive goes slowly down the tracks. He can see at the top of the trees a jagged fine line of the horizon. More coal is shoveled into the furnace for more power to the steam engine, as it gets progressively on its way. Before the train can build up enough steam to have the more rapid rolling, from out of the brush comes an individual, running fast, faster and faster. He is running alongside of the linked train cars at its middle. The rocky ground under his feet almost causes him to fall, and slow him down some. But still he is able to maintain a steady pace alongside of the train. Then a hand goes up and grabs the iron ladder. Gripping tight, he heaves up with fast moving legs and feet, thrusting his body upward to jump and climb aboard. And now, clinched to the iron ladder with his bundle tucked and squeezed underneath one elbow, he is hanging on. A new beginner Hobo Clarence Taylor makes his way to the top of the boxcar and gets down on one knee.

Now he can see the same jagged horizon as the engineer. But his heart's pounding at its biggest amazement. And the cold wind is hitting against his face. But adrenalin and the blood flowing make the cold chill just a breezy wind, rather than freezing him out. So Clarence gets aboard without being seen. He collects himself and takes the next step, which is to go back down the ladder and leap into the open boxcar. He approaches the ladder duck-walking, and has the bundle tucked and held tight in one hand. Closer and closer with every step he takes. Finally he is at the top of the ladder. But the train is moving fast now, and has the ground swift, sweeping underneath as the train cars pass. Hesitant, Clarence is able to get a leg up and plant it down on a couple of steps beyond. His other leg follows and gets the next step. He is hugged in close to the ladder and has his bundle held tight against himself. Slowly, he comes down the ladder with the harsh wind pushing against him. And still hanging on tight, without being seen; The train is rumbling and swaying from side to side with a big motion from its oversize load. Hanging on edge, Clarence is able to reach out with the hand that has the bundle, and tosses it inside. Then he leaps from off the ladder down into the moving boxcar. He is unable to remain on his feet, and tumbles down to a rough landing. Then he gets up and turns about looking out at the country side. It's as though he's in another dimension of time and space. His feelings and emotions are all so very exciting and new. Yet there's paranoia too, that has the moment not all together so very good.

www.ingramcontent.com/pod-product-compliance
Ingram Content Group UK Ltd.
Pitfield, Milton Keynes, MK11 3LW, UK
UKHW021050270726
13967UKWH00012B/200

9 781412 061773